KT-556-613

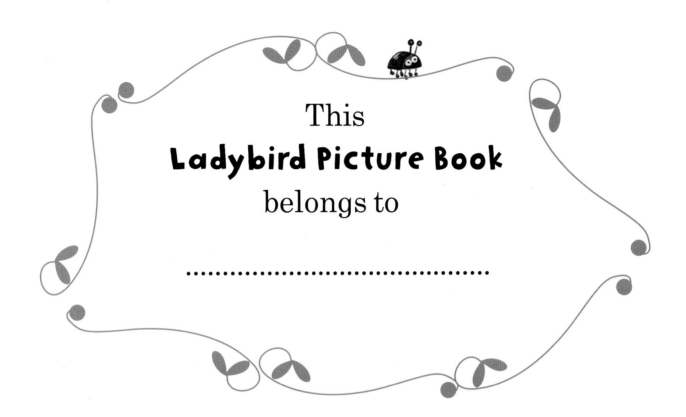

This
Ladybird Picture Book
belongs to

....

LADYBIRD BOOKS

UK | USA | Canada | Ireland | Australia
India | New Zealand | South Africa
Ladybird Books is part of the Penguin Random House group of companies
whose addresses can be found at global.penguinrandomhouse.com.

www.penguin.co.uk   www.puffin.co.uk   www.ladybird.co.uk

Penguin
Random House
UK

First published 1999
Reissued 2012 as part of the Ladybird First Favourite Tales series
This Ladybird Picture Books edition published 2019
001

Copyright © Ladybird Books Ltd, 1999, 2012, 2019

Printed in China
A CIP catalogue record for this book is available from the British Library

ISBN: 978–0–241–38432–9

All correspondence to:
Ladybird Books, Penguin Random House Children's
80 Strand, London WC2R 0RL

MIX
Paper from
responsible sources
FSC
www.fsc.org
FSC® C018179

Ladybird Picture Books

The Little Red Hen

BASED ON A TRADITIONAL FOLK TALE

retold by Rone Randall ★ illustrated by Ailie Busby

One sunny spring morning, the little red hen was scratching about the farmyard.

Suddenly …
"Look! Look!" clucked the little red hen.
"I spy …"

"…an ear of corn!"
The little red hen was very excited! She
showed it to her friends in the farmyard.
"Who will help me to plant this corn?"
she asked.

"Not I," yawned the sleepy, stripy cat.
"Not I," sniffed the sleek, skinny rat.
"Not I," snorted the plump, pink pig.

"Then I will plant this corn myself,"
said the little red hen.

And she did.

The little red hen weeded and watered the corn every day.

Soon the corn began to grow.

It grew... and it grew...

...and it **grew** till it was tall and golden.

"Who will help me to cut the corn?" asked the little red hen.
"Not I," purred the preening, stripy cat.
"Not I," sang the snoozing, skinny rat.
"Not I," mumbled the muddy, pink pig.

Too busy!

"Then I will cut the corn myself,"
said the little red hen.

And she did.

"Who will help me to take this corn to the mill?" asked the little red hen.
"Not I," said the big, stripy cat.
"Not I," shouted the small, skinny rat.
"Not I," laughed the large, pink pig.

Too busy!

"Then I will take this corn to the mill myself," said the little red hen.

And she did.

Round and round went the windmill as it ground the corn.

Soon the little red hen had a big sack of fine white flour to take home. She was very pleased!

"Who will help me to bake some bread?"
asked the little red hen.
"Not I," called the curled-up, stripy cat.
"Not I," said the sneaky, skinny rat.
"Not I," giggled the gleeful, pink pig.

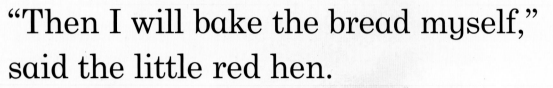

"Then I will bake the bread myself,"
said the little red hen.

And she did.

"Who will help me to eat this bread?"
asked the little red hen.

"I will!" said the eager, stripy cat.
"It smells so-o-o delicious!"
"I will!" said the hungry, skinny rat.
"I love freshly baked bread!"
"I will!" said the greedy, pink pig.
"With lots of creamy butter, please!"

But the little red hen had other plans.
"Not you, stripy cat! Not you, skinny rat!
Not you, greedy pig! You didn't help me at
all. So now I'm going to eat this warm,
fresh bread all by myself."

And she did ... with *oodles* of creamy butter!

Ladybird Picture Books

Look out for...

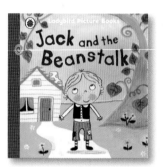
Jack and the Beanstalk

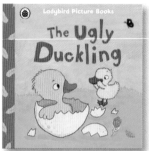
The Ugly Duckling

The Enormous Turnip

Goldilocks

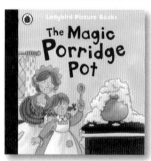
The Magic Porridge Pot

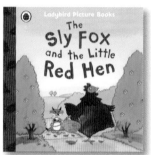
The Sly Fox and the Little Red Hen

Hansel and Gretel

Cinderella

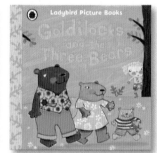
Goldilocks and the Three Bears

The Three Billy Goats Gruff

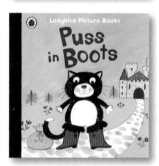
Puss in Boots

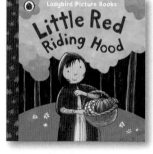
Little Red Riding Hood

The Wizard of Oz

The Little Red Hen

The Gingerbread Man

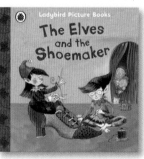
Alice in Wonderland

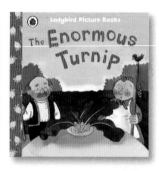
The Elves and the Shoemaker